Growing God's Kids

KEEPING YOUR COOL

A Book about Anger

CAROLYN LARSEN
ILLUSTRATED BY TIM O'CONNOR

BakerBooks
a division of Baker Publishing Group
Grand Rapids, Michigan

T0366933

Text © 2016 by Carolyn Larsen
Illustrations © 2016 by Baker Publishing Group

Published by Baker Books
a division of Baker Publishing Group
P.O. Box 6287, Grand Rapids, MI 49516-6287
www.bakerbooks.com

Printed in the United States of America

Library of Congress Cataloging-in-Publication Data
Names: Larsen, Carolyn, 1950– author.
Title: Keeping your cool : a book about anger / Carolyn Larsen ;
    illustrated by Tim O'Connor.
Description: Grand Rapids : Baker Books, 2016. | Series:
    Growing God's kids
Identifiers: LCCN 2015047245 | ISBN 9780801009129 (pbk.)
Subjects: LCSH: Anger—Religious aspects—Christianity—
    Juvenile literature. | Anger in children—Religious aspects—
    Christianity—Juvenile literature.
Classification: LCC BV4627.A5 L37 2016 | DDC 241/.3—dc23
LC record available at https://lccn.loc.gov/2015047245

Scripture quotations are from The Living Bible, copyright © 1971. Used by permission of Tyndale House Publishers, Inc., Carol Stream, Illinois 60188. All rights reserved.

22   23   24   25   8   7   6   5

Stop your anger! . . .
Don't fret and worry—
it only leads to harm.

———

PSALM 37:8

See that boy? That's Max. He gets angry a lot.

My name is Leonard, and I'm Max's favorite toy.

Sometimes when Max is making a village with blocks, his little brother Zach wrecks it all. When the buildings go flying, Max gets angry. He throws blocks across the room and yells at his brother for messing up his village.

Max's mom is not happy when he behaves that way. She reminds Max that Zach is little. He didn't mean to wreck Max's village.

She tells Max, "Pick up all the toys, even the ones Zach knocked down. Then you must tell Zach you're sorry for yelling."

Everyone gets angry sometimes. The problem is how Max acts when he is angry. Then Mom says, "Here are some ideas of what you could do when you're angry."

- You could count to ten before you say a word or do anything.
- You could grab a pillow and squeeze it.
- After you calm down you could ask Zach not to wreck your toys.
- You could play with Zach.

Stop your anger!
Psalm 37:8

riday night is family movie night. Max's mom makes popcorn, and everyone has a lot of fun. (I like when they watch superhero movies.)

But Max gets angry when he doesn't get to choose the movie. He's so angry that he dumps his bowl of popcorn on his sister's head. Max ruins the fun for everyone.

His mom and dad send him to his room. "You don't get to watch the movie at all, and you're grounded from TV for the whole next day," they tell him.

Max is going to miss his favorite Saturday cartoons.

Later, Dad tells Max that no one gets his own way all the time. "You must learn how to be nice when you don't get your way. No pouting. No whining."

Dad promises to make a chart showing that each child gets a turn to choose the family movie.

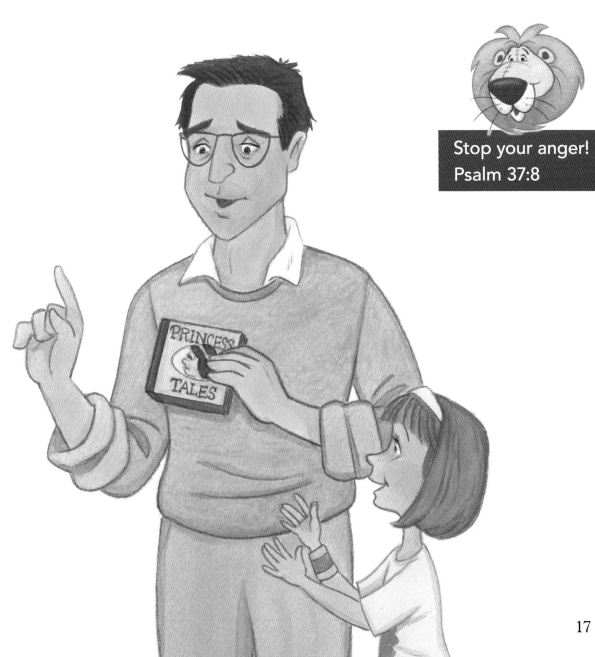

Stop your anger!
Psalm 37:8

17

When Zach bops Max on the head with a laser sword, Max forgets that Zach is little.

He gets angry and hits Zach back harder.

Mom doesn't think that's OK and puts Max in time-out.

"Tell Zach you're sorry for hitting him," she says.

"When someone hits you, you may want to hit back. But hitting back just starts a bigger fight."

Mom tells Max that hitting is not OK. Ever. "You could just walk away when Zach hits you, or you could ask Zach to be more careful. Tell Zach you don't like to be hit."

Stop your anger!
Psalm 37:8

Max likes to play with friends. But he wants to choose what they play. His friends like soccer. Sometimes Max doesn't want to play soccer, so he gets angry. He kicks the ball across the field, stomps his foot, and shouts at his friends.

Max's friends don't want to play with him when he acts that way.

They leave to go play soccer with other friends, and Max is all by himself.

Dad tells Max, "It's OK to have favorite things to do. But remember, other people have favorite things too. Instead of getting angry when someone else chooses, you should take turns and let others choose sometimes."

Stop your anger!
Psalm 37:8

29

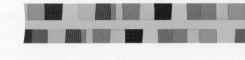

What could I do the next time my brother or sister makes me angry?

1. Walk away.

2. Count to ten.

3. Calm down: then ask them not to do what was bothering me.

What can I do when I don't get my way?

1. Understand that it's fair to take turns.

2. Remember that others have favorite things too.

3. Just be quiet and do what the other person wants to do.

What should I do when someone hits me?

1. Count to ten.

2. Walk away.

3. Tell the person that I don't like to be hit.

When my friends don't do what I want, I could . . .

1. Agree to do what they want this time.
2. Play with someone else.
3. Suggest another game, but go along with what most of the people want to do.

Remember

God says not to let anger control you because when something is controlling you it decides how you act and what you say. (See Ephesians 4:26–27.)

God says that losing your temper and behaving badly mean you are acting foolish. (See Proverbs 29:11.)

God says to be the person who stops the fight, not the one who makes it worse. (See Proverbs 15:18.)

God says to listen to other people sometimes instead of getting angry. Others have good ideas too. (See James 1:19–20.)

It's OK that you get angry sometimes—everyone does. What's important is how you act when you're angry. Ask God to help you learn to act like his child.

Stop your anger!
Psalm 37:8